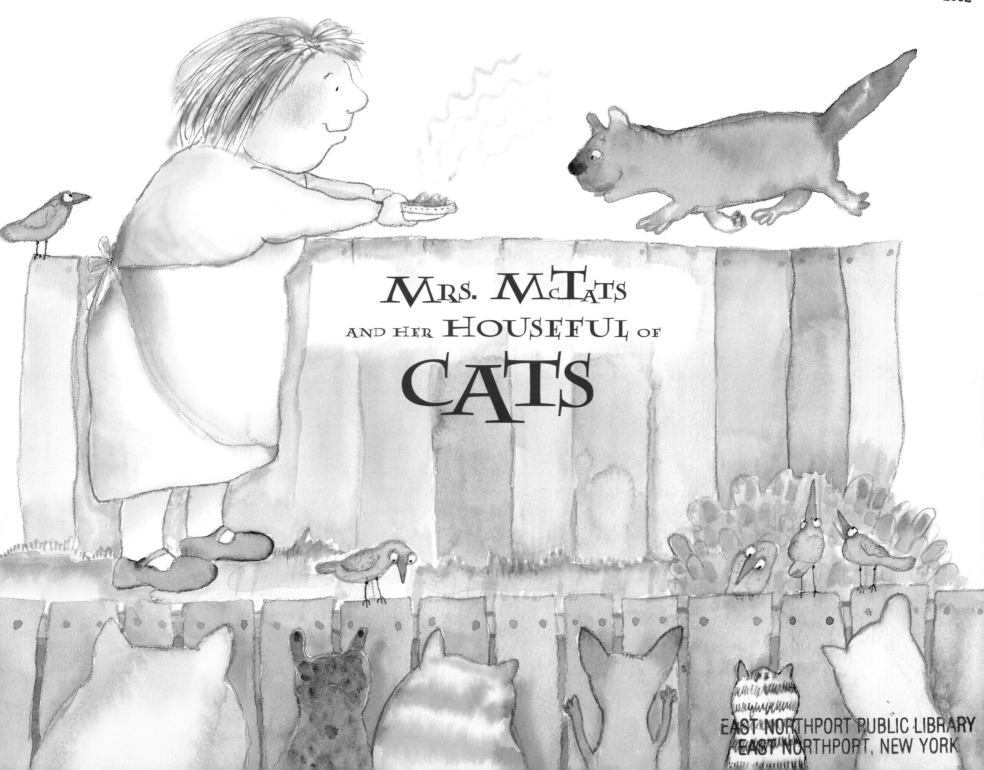

Mrs. McTats
AND HER HOUSEFUL OF
CATS

Mrs. McTats
and her Houseful of
Cats

by Alyssa Satin Capucilli

with illustrations by Joan Rankin

Margaret K. McElderry Books

NEW YORK   LONDON   TORONTO   SYDNEY   SINGAPORE

Margaret K. McElderry Books
An imprint of Simon & Schuster Children's Publishing Division
1230 Avenue of the Americas
New York, NY 10020

Book design by Ann Bobco.
The text of this book is set in Adobe Caslon.
The illustrations are rendered in watercolor.

Printed in Hong Kong

10 9 8 7 6 5 4

Library of Congress Cataloging-in-Publication Data
Capucilli, Alyssa Satin.
Mrs. McTats and her houseful of cats / Alyssa Satin Capucilli; illustrations by Joan Rankin.—1st ed.
p.   cm.
Summary: A woman with a single cat named Abner makes room for twenty-four more cats and a puppy she names Zoom.
ISBN 0-689-83185-4
[1. Cats—Fiction. 2. Alphabet. 3. Counting. 4. Stories in rhyme.] I. Rankin, Joan, ill. II. Title.
PZ8.3.C1935Mr   2001   [E]—dc21   99-34962

For a sweet dear named Liza
—A. S. C.

To Tony, who never turned any cats
away
—J. R.

In a small, cozy cottage
lived Mrs. McTats.
She lived all alone,
except for one cat.

Every morning she left
as the clock struck eight—
"To market, to market!
I mustn't be late."

She browsed through the market
and chose a plump fish.
"For **A**bner and me.
What a sumptuous dish!"

But when she got home,
there came a scratch on the door,
and in walked two cats.
Was there room for two more?

"Come in, my sweet dears,"
said Mrs. McTats.
"I'm sure I've got room
for just two more cats.

I'll call you Basil,

and Curly you'll be.

I only had one cat,
but now I have three!"

The very next morning
Mrs. McTats woke early.
She stopped to pet **A**bner
and **B**asil and **C**urly.

"To market, to market!
I mustn't be late.

This chicken, I think,
will surely taste great."

But when she got home,
there came a scratch on the door,
and in walked three cats.
Was there room for three more?

"Come in, my sweet dears,"
said Mrs. McTats.
"I think I've got room
for just three more cats.

Now, give me a moment.
What shall your names be?

You're **D**olly,

you're **E**rnest,

and **F**uzzy makes three!"

The very next morning
off went Mrs. McTats.
"What can I buy
for my six hungry cats?"

"I've got it!" she said.
"I'll make a nice stew."
So she carried home beef
and liver to brew.

But back at home
there came a scratch on the door,
and in walked four cats.
Was there room for four more?

"Come in, my sweet dears,"
said Mrs. McTats.
"I know there's a place
for just four more cats.
Ten's a fine number—
ten cats and me—

I'll call you Goldie

and Herman
you'll be."

Izzy

and **J**ezebel

pranced 'cross the floor.
And then, right behind them . . .

. . . followed five more!

"Koko

and Linus,

Millie,

Noreen.

And you shall be Oscar.

There, that makes fifteen!"

The very next day,
off went Mrs. McTats.
"What can I possibly
feed fifteen cats?"

She chose a fresh tuna.

She chose a fine trout.

But when she got home,
her cats were all out!

She counted her cats
from one to fifteen,
but somehow six more cats
had just joined the scene!
"Come, come, my sweet dears,"
said Mrs. McTats.
"I'm sure I have plenty
for twenty-one cats.

Pip,

Quip,

and Rosebud.

Sally

and Toesie.

Ursula, dear,
do make yourself cozy."

But then came another
scratch on the door.

Could it be more cats?
How many more?

In came **V**iolet.

In came **W**innie.

And, just behind,
a kitten she named **X**innie.

In came 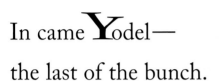Yodel—

the last of the bunch.

Twenty-five cats
ready for lunch!

But something was missing.
What could it be?
Just what it was,
Mrs. McTats could not see.
As she stood there puzzling,
there was a scratch on the door
and Mrs. McTats wondered,
Could there really be more?
Could she squeeze in more cats?
More than twenty-five?
Who was the one
who was next to arrive?

"Come in, my sweet dear,"
said Mrs. McTats.
"I live in this cottage with
twenty-five cats.
But if you don't mind,
you're welcome to stay.
You're welcome to eat.
You're welcome to play."

Now in that small cottage
lives Mrs. McTats,
all happy and cozy with her
twenty-five cats . . .

. . . and one little puppy,
who's known as Zoom,
in a small, cozy cottage
with plenty of room.

And just when the clock
strikes each morning at eight,
Mrs. McTats hurries off.
"I mustn't be late!

To market, to market!
What treats will there be?
For twenty-six sweet dears
from A to Z!"